This Meno book belongs to:

ADVENTURE OF meno

BY TONY & ANGELA DITERLIZZI

Book One
BIG FUN!

Presented in Vibrant Meno-Color!

SIMON & SCHUSTER BOOKS FOR YOUNG READERS
NEW YORK   LONDON   TORONTO   SYDNEY

It is sunshine time
at the house of Meno.
But where is Meno?

Meno!

Please to meet Meno!
But where is Yamagoo?

Not here.

Not here.

Not here.

Where?

Yamagoo!

Meno,
what do we eat
for sunshine snack?

We enjoy moo juice . . .

. . . and dough with hole.

Hip-hooray!

Okay.
Now is time
for a BIG FUN!

Meno,
what is
a BIG FUN?

Silly Yamagoo.
You know what is
a BIG FUN!

Hee-hee!

Tee-hee!

Every fun is
a BIG FUN
with Meno!

Pronounce Menu

 Meno: MEE-no

 Yamagoo: YA-ma-goo

Meno-Speak

 big fun: funniest thing ever

 dough with hole: doughnut

 moo juice: milk

 sunshine snack: breakfast

 sunshine time: morning

ADVENTURE OF meno

PLANETMENO.COM

SIMON & SCHUSTER BOOKS FOR YOUNG READERS
An imprint of Simon & Schuster Children's Publishing Division
1230 Avenue of the Americas, New York, New York 10020

Book design by Tony, Angela, and Lizzy B.
The text for this book is set in Futura, Secret Recipe, and Square Meal.
The illustrations for this book are rendered with magic.
Big thanks to Joe for the inspiration
Manufactured in China
2 4 6 8 10 9 7 5 3 1
Library of Congress Cataloging-in-Publication Data
DiTerlizzi, Tony.
Big fun! / by Tony and Angela DiTerlizzi. — 1st ed.
p. cm. — (Adventure of Meno ; bk. 1)
Summary: After eating breakfast, good friends Meno the space alien
and Yamagoo the jellyfish make time for fun.
ISBN: 978-1-4169-7148-1 (hardcover : alk. paper)
[1. Extraterrestrial beings—Fiction. 2. Jellyfishes—Fiction. 3. Friendship—Fiction.] I. Title.
PZ7.D629Bi 2009
[E]—dc22
2008015202

MENO THEME SONG

(To the tune of "Twinkle, Twinkle, Little Star")

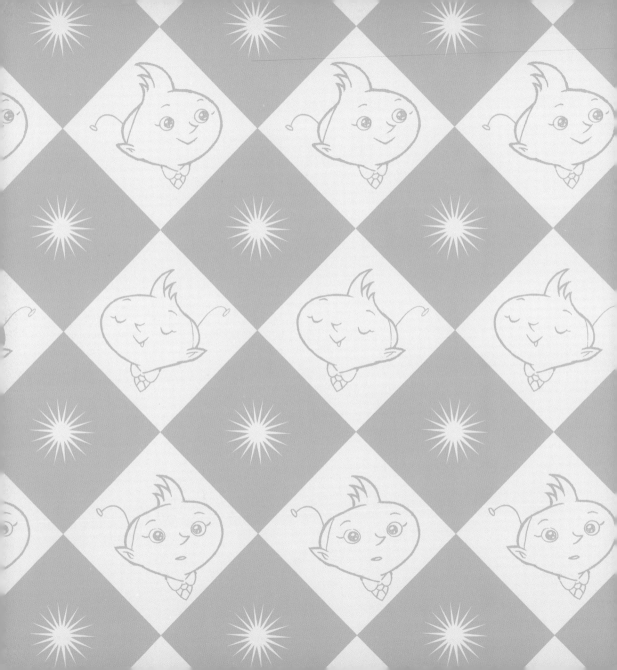